JAZZ OWLS

ALSO BY MARGARITA ENGLE

Soaring Earth:
A Companion Memoir to Enchanted Air

Forest World

Aire encantado:
Dos culturas, dos alas: una memoria

Lion Island:
Cuba's Warrior of Words

Enchanted Air:
Two Cultures, Two Wings: A Memoir

Silver People:
Voices from the Panama Canal

The Lightning Dreamer:
Cuba's Greatest Abolitionist

The Wild Book

Hurricane Dancers:
The First Caribbean Pirate Shipwreck

The Firefly Letters:
A Suffragette's Journey to Cuba

Tropical Secrets:
Holocaust Refugees in Cuba

The Surrender Tree:
Poems of Cuba's Struggle for Freedom

The Poet Slave of Cuba:
A Biography of Juan Francisco Manzano

JAZZ OWLS

A Novel
of the
Zoot
Suit
Riots

MARGARITA ENGLE

Art by
RUDY GUTIERREZ

atheneum New York London Toronto Sydney New Delhi

Para Sandra Ríos Balderrama, héroe de las bibliotecas
and for dancers, dreamers, and heroes of peace,
in honor of all the nonviolent Chicano protesters of later decades,
whose courage triumphed despite vicious attacks against their
communities in the 1940s.

atheneum

An imprint of Simon & Schuster Children's Publishing Division • 1230 Avenue of the Americas, New York, New York 10020 • This book is a work of fiction. Any references to historical events, real people, or real places are used fictitiously. Other names, characters, places, and events are products of the author's imagination, and any resemblance to actual events or places or persons, living or dead, is entirely coincidental. • Text copyright © 2018 by Margarita Engle • Illustrations copyright © 2018 by Rudy Gutierrez • All rights reserved, including the right of reproduction in whole or in part in any form. • Atheneum logo is a trademark of Simon & Schuster, Inc. • For information about special discounts for bulk purchases, please contact Simon & Schuster Special Sales at 1-866-506-1949 or business@simonandschuster.com. • The Simon & Schuster Speakers Bureau can bring authors to your live event. For more information or to book an event, contact the Simon & Schuster Speakers Bureau at 1-866-248-3049 or visit our website at www.simonspeakers.com. • Also available in an Atheneum hardcover edition • Book design by Debra Sfetsios-Conover • The text for this book was set in Weiss Std. • The illustrations for this book were rendered in mixed media (acrylic paint, pencils and ink). • Manufactured in the United States of America • First Atheneum paperback edition August 2019 • 10 9 8 7 6 5 4 3 2 1 • The Library of Congress has cataloged the hardcover edition as follows: • Names: Engle, Margarita, author. | Gutierrez, Rudy, illustrator. • Title: Jazz owls : a novel of the Zoot Suit Riots / Margarita Engle ; illustrated by Rudy Gutierrez. • Description: First edition. | New York : Atheneum Books for Young Readers, [2018] | Summary: In early 1940s Los Angeles, Mexican Americans Marisela and Lorena work in canneries all day then jitterbug with sailors all night with their zoot suit wearing younger brother, Ray, as escort until the night racial violence leads to murder. Includes historical note. | Includes bibliographical references. | • Identifiers: LCCN 2017024247 (print) | LCCN 2017038525 (eBook) • ISBN 9781534409439 (hardcover) | ISBN 9781534409446 (pbk) | ISBN 9781534409453 (eBook) | Subjects: LCSH: Zoot Suit Riots, Los Angeles, Calif., 1943—Juvenile fiction. | CYAC: Novels in verse. | Zoot Suit Riots, Los Angeles, Calif., 1943—Fiction. | Race relations—Fiction. | Dancing—Fiction. | Sailors—Fiction. | Mexican Americans—Fiction. | World War, 1939-1945—United States—Fiction. | Los Angeles (Calif.)—History—20th century—Fiction. • Classification: LCC PZ7.5.E54 (eBook) | LCC PZ7.5.E54 Jaz 2018 (print) | DDC [Fic]—dc23 • LC record available at https://lccn.loc.gov/2017024247

Pero una nueva pulsación, un nuevo latido
arroja al río de la calle nuevos sedientes seres.
Se cruzan, se entrecruzan y suben.
Vuelan a ras de tierra.

But a new pulse, a new throb
hurls thirsty new beings into the river of the street.
They cross, crisscross, and rise.
They fly close to earth.

—**Xavier Villaurrutia**,
from *Nocturno de Los Angeles*
(*Los Angeles Nocturne*)

CONTENTS

THE RIVER OF MUSIC

Los Angeles, California

August 1942

Manolito from Cuba
Age 16

We flow into the city of *ángeles*
following a flood of young sailors—
thousands at first, then millions
from all over the U.S., scared teens
who long to dance, need to leap,
craving that feeling of being so alive
as they pass through L.A.
on their swift way
to the horrors
of war.

I'm just one of hundreds of musicians
who arrive from New York, Memphis, Chicago,
Kansas City, Saint Louis, and from the steamy islands
of *música* too, Cuba and Puerto Rico, drummers,
trumpeters, and saxophonists, wizards of rhythm,
wearing our loose suits, the zoot shape
that drapes us to keep dance leaps smooth
and COOL in this HOT summer river
of JAZZ!

SWIMMING
SEASON

August 1942

Jazz Craze!

Marisela

Age 16

The musicians call us owls
because we're patriotic girls
who stay up LATE after working all day,
so we can DANCE with young sailors
who are on their way
to triumph
or death
on distant
ocean waves.

I love feeling jazz-winged,
so this owl life is easy for me,
until early morning, when my shift
at the cannery begins, right after a LONG journey
of clanging streetcar bells and SLEEPY smiles, all
those memories of dancing the jitterbug, Lindy Hop,
and jump blues, while adding my own swaying bit
of Latin-style swing rhythm!
¡RITMO!

Sweaty

Lorena

Age 14

Everyone says I'm still the calm, sensible one,
even though I quit school two years ago,
right after a teacher washed my mouth out
with foamy
foul-tasting
soap.

My crime? Speaking words the teacher
called dog language—*español*,
my family's natural *música*,
the songlike rhythm and melody
of lovely syllables from Mazatlán in México,
where Mami and Papá once danced
beside warm, sparkling, tropical
ocean waves.

I don't like staying up all night with Marisela,
because our day shift at the cannery means sleep
is needed, to keep fingers alert so they don't
get crushed by machinery
or sliced
by knives.

High heels, wide skirt, jitterbug
and all that jazz, the sailors call us owls
because we obey the U.S. government's wish
for a sizzling, sweaty summer of pre-death
entertainment, to cheer navy recruits while they wait
for their warships, our battles, this shared war
of worldwide violence.

Chaperoned by our brother—that's the only way
any *mexicana* mother will allow her daughters
to dance, joining las *señoritas de la* USO
—*la Organización de* Service United—
a club where navy boys swing and hop before gliding
out toward the oceanic unknown.

Our older brother, Nicolás, is already over there
somewhere in Europe, Asia, or maybe the South Pacific.
We're not even allowed to know the name of the land
where he's fighting against fascism and racial hatred.

So Marisela and I have to depend on little Ray
to escort us safely from our exhausting cannery jobs
to an evening of dutiful, patriotic dancing.
Everyone says I'm sensible, but secretly I feel
really angry.

¡Mira!

Ray
Age 12

Swing dance, swing shift, swing a bat,
swings at the park, swing from a tree—
isn't it funny how many meanings
one little five-*letra* word can hold?

That's why I wear my clothes BIG.
HUGE suit, ZOOT suit, baggy pants
for a leaping dance, COOL hat, WIDE shoulders,
watcha—mira—LOOK at me, not old enough
to DIE in the war, but plenty *GRANDE*
when I perform my own style of *pachuco* hop
at the All Nations Club, where I go alone
after taking *las* owls
to the USO.

As long as my sisters don't get in trouble,
Mami lets me stay out, so we can all be patriots
like our superhero **BRAVE**
big brother.

Impatient
Marisela

Cannery work is all about seasons,
and August means *duraznos*,
so I have to DANCE with my dress
full of peach fuzz and the sweet-smelling juice
that leaves sticky stains under my fingernails.

Only men like Papá get the best packing jobs,
cooking thick syrups, sealing slick cans,
and carrying heavy boxes to earn
a better living, while women and girls
have to do piecework,
prep work,
knife work,
slice, slice, slice,
sliding this sharp blade
through soft fruit flesh
ALL DAY.

Checkers watch us.
They fire us if we're caught working
too slowly or too quickly,
because slow means lazy
but swift means we'll make TOO MUCH money.

Imagine that. . . .

Rápido, rápido, the silenced half of my bilingual voice
longs to shout, let this day of rapid peach slicing END
so I can finally go out to *el baile*, the LIVELY dance
where my real life BEGINS, all those owl hours
of stomping heels and flying LEAPS,
energetic movements—my only true FREEDOM!

Despacio, slow down, sensible Lorenita reminds me.
If we get fired, Papá will be ashamed, and Mami
won't let us leave the house, so try to keep a steady pace,
remember it's not a peach-slicing race, just chop
smooth and easy, like the fox-trot that tired sailors
always request when they need a slower,
more restful
dance step.

At the end of my workday, I try to relax
and remind myself that if I slip on this peach-juicy floor,
I'll be fired, so I STROLL like an old woman, carefully
ESCAPING!

Censored
Lorena

Maybe I should have stayed in school,
because Spanish is forbidden here at work, too.

Ray mixes his words back and forth
or makes up completely new ones, like *watcha*,
and let's eat a picnic *lonche* at noon,
or look at all those *trocas* in the *parqueadero* lot.

When he does that, I feel so old-fashioned,
even though we're only two years apart.
Español at home, English while standing
at this conveyor belt, watching peaches roll
past me like quiet slices of time,
I can't let myself forget
that being revealed as *bilingüe*
is a sure way to get fired.

Checkers don't like two-language girls
because they start to wonder what we'll say
about them, so we have to choose *el inglés*
or joblessness.

In Trouble
Ray

I shouldn't have gone
to that party at the Williams Ranch
after taking my owl sisters to the USO.

It was just some girl's birthday
until a fight broke out, and then later
these guys from 38th Street went back to take
revenge
against rowdies
from Downey.

All I did was swim in the farm pond.
How can anyone blame me—this is summer,
crazy hot, *loco* sweaty, and public pools
let *mexicanos* jump in only on certain Fridays,
right before the janitor drains all that water.
Yeah, man, *fíjate*, fix your mind on THAT!
THEY believe OUR skin is DIRTY!
Well, I think THEIR brains are *sucios*,
because racial hatred is the WORST filth
on Earth—in fact, it must be this blaze
of swimming weather that fried
that first policeman's hate-filled mind

and made him act
estúpido.

But this second cop is even more idiotic,
dumb as *un buey*,
a slow ox. . . .
Hold still so I can hit you again, he commands
over and over—sit down, shut up, accept
the sort of truth only a grown man's fist
can offer—but he's wasting words,
because his thumping knuckles
are all I hear now,
drowning   the   sound
    of insults
                as   I   fade
in and out
        of caring.

Ambitious

Reporter #1

This lurid murder at that swimming hole
is just the thing I need to make my name
famous!

Most of these foreign kids quit school
after fifth grade or eighth, just to work
in factories or canneries, so they can pay
for those fancy zoot suits that use up
too much valuable cloth; it's an outrage
in wartime, the way they wear baggy pants
instead of narrow ones, wasting fabric
that our military needs for uniforms
and hospital sheets.

The Mexican Problem, that's what I really
need to write about, but which angle?
Zoot suits that imitate the sleek style of black musicians?
Or stubborn foreign mothers who refuse
to let their kids learn English, fit in, look right,
act regular, assimilate, change into real
Americans . . . ?

Maybe I'll go for this police crackdown story
first and then try switching to the bad-mother angle

only if I find a fantastic example of a Latin family
that talks normal
and eats
ordinary food—burgers
instead of spicy
tacos.

Yeah, that's my plan, but only if this steamy
summer murder
fails to make
the front page
over and over,
the way I hope it will,
considering the eerie name
of that swimming hole—
Sleepy Lagoon!

Aggressive
Reporter #2

Hah!
Other reporters think they'll scoop me,
but I'm already here on the Williams Ranch
in Eastside, where some foreigner called José Díaz
was found bleeding, right before he went
to the hospital
and died.

Stabbed, beaten, robbed—that's news!
Sleepy Lagoon—it's the perfect headline.
Sounds so peaceful and pretty,
but it's spooky enough to make readers
shiver—chills up the spine, that's what sells
newspapers!

The Shadow of José Díaz
Ray

I wonder if the man who got knifed
is really a spirit in heaven now, like Lorena says,
or just a lonely ghost floating above frog songs
and slimy algae, the way Marisela warns
when she tells me not to fight back
if I ever get jumped on the street.

I could map that crime scene in my mind.
Seven farm labor shacks north of the lagoon,
and seven south—*mexicanos*, Chinese—and that empty
little house where the Hakada family used to live,
until they were taken away and locked up
just for being Japanese.

¡*Watcha*! Look at ME, try to **SEE** who I really AM,
americano just like you two cops who keep beating me—
American and Mexican at the same time, like Nico,
my brother, a HERO who FIGHTS for OUR
SHARED country, these UNITED States.
Where's the UNITY?

A Waste of Time
Policeman #1

The governor of this great state of California
ordered a crackdown on Eastside boys.
Mexicans, in other words.

So the Los Angeles district attorney's office
said we should go ahead and do it, and now
here we are, grown men
beating up little kids
who don't know
what
or why.

Not Me
Ray

Gangster? No way!
Zooter, sure, but dance cat
and outlaw are two different things,
one violent, the other just drape-shaped
COOL.

A Gang of Children?
Policeman #2

BABY GANGSTERS is the silliest headline
I've ever seen, but newspaper reporters
are powerful people, so I go out and smile
when I'm supposed to, then frown on cue,
have my picture taken,
and try to put on a show
of being the strong, silent type,
like a modern-day cowboy in a uniform,
conquering Aztec warriors and other
Hollywood bad guys. . . .

Well, sure, I know they're not actually
building sacrificial pyramids, but what if Mexico
really is like Japan, just waiting to attack
the rest of us—then the headline
BABY GANGSTERS makes sense, doesn't it?
Some of these Mexican kids
with Indian blood
almost look Asian.

Arrested?
Mami

¿*Las muchachas también?* The girls, too,
after you've taken my boy?

Pero mis hijas are so well behaved, *se portan bien,*
son señoritas de la USO. *Tecolotes*—owls. *¿No?*
¿Cómo que you don't understand what I mean?

After all that patriotic dancing,
you newspaper liars and crooked police
still don't think *mexicana* girls deserve
respect?

Marisela and Lorenita are not even tough
like those others, *las zooterinas*, the ones
who wear
big hair
and boys' pants.

Disgusted
Papá

I was born right here
in California, and only went to Mazatlán
when my grandparents were old
and needed help.

I met my wife there, brought her back here,
and now our U.S.-born children are treated
like invaders.

You'd think the way Nicolás
is risking his life for this country
would be enough of a show of loyalty
to help him earn appreciation
for our whole *familia*.

We work hard!
All the farms and canneries would be empty
without us, and guess who—yes, you—
all the policemen and reporters would be
hungry!

Hundreds of Suspects
Marisela

Rounded up like *vacas*—cows—
handcuffed, LOCKED UP, boys, girls,
mostly Mexicans, but black neighbors too.

Did they arrest me just because Ray
was at that party, or because anyone
who ever goes anywhere near *la* 38th Street
is being scooped up for this *policía* game
of finding someone to BLAME
for the murder
of a stranger?

We didn't know José Díaz!
We weren't at that Sleepy Lagoon party.
We don't know anything about killing.
We're USO owls, we DANCE and work,
that's all.
Eso es todo.
Yes, I'm DONE
talking.

Photographed
Lorena

I always hoped a burst of light
from flashing cameras might reach me
during the Orange Queen beauty contest,
or a graduation ceremony for some
fancy secretarial school.

But I'm a slightly darker brown than Marisela,
so she would probably be the winner of any pageant
judged by old Hollywood men, and I'll never
make it through a private school, unless
I somehow manage to keep my cannery job
long enough to save for tuition.

So instead here we are, sisters, *hermanas*,
shoulder to shoulder, standing in this lineup,
hands behind our backs, flash, flash, flash,
scary cameras. . . .

Most of the arrested girls
are *zooterinas* wearing boys' drapes—
baggy pants and fingertip jackets,
hair piled high
to make them look tall
and strong.

In my homemade flour-sack dress,
I begin to realize why Ray always tries
to look stylish.

It would feel safe to know that policemen
are just as scared of kids who swagger
in zoot clothes
as we are
of their shiny guns
and dazzling
flash, flash
cameras.

If I can't alarm these cops with my confident
way of walking,
maybe I can at least shock them with lawyerlike
calmness.

Trapped
Ray

It took me a long time to perfect
this *gato*-cat
hipster-*vato*
cool-*pachuco*
way of walking—relaxed
shoulder hunch, squared
boxer arms,
easy
runner knees,
swaying through time,
CLAIMING my share
of rugged public
sidewalk.

A tough strut is proof that I'm demanding
my own powerful
slice
of space . . .
but when I slow-walk into that trial room
I'm just one of so many older boys
who are faking the same coolness,
so nobody
notices
ME.

Boiling-hot mad and terrified, I barely listen
to the row of lawyers who try to organize
all of us
alphabetically.

They start with our second last names—
our mothers' *apellidos*—instead of our fathers'
surnames, until someone corrects them,
and finally they manage to see
that Montes del Río
doesn't just mean "mountains
of the river," it's Papá's father's last name
FOLLOWED by Mami's father's last name,
NOT the other way around.

I end up lounging in the middle of a long,
snaking circle of suspects
that rings
this big, frightening official room.

Shiny hair. Ducktail cuts. Slicked back.
It's the way we look that got us arrested
in the first place, and now
no amount of coolness
can help us.

The grand jury will see us
with dirty shirts
and oily hair
because jail guards
won't let us change
into clean clothes
or get barbered to look military
like newspaper HEROES—like Nico,
if he's still
ALIVE.

Wolf Pack
Reporter #1

There's no telling whether the verdicts
would be different without our headlines.
What if these teenagers had been allowed
to change their clothes and wash their hair?

No matter—all but a couple dozen boys
have already been sent home for lack of evidence,
after their mothers raged at the jailhouse,
shouting in Spanish and English,
demanding to know where, why, how. . . .

Yeah, those tough foreign women are a story
of their own, but for now I'll just stick to these
surefire scary headlines, like:
PROWLING WOLVES OF SLEEPY LAGOON.

The real name of this trial is *People v. Zammora*,
which sounds about as exciting as one more sad
Hollywood movie star divorce.
Yawn.

Citizens' Committee for the Defense of Mexican American Youth

Reporter #2

I couldn't dream up a more boring headline
than the name of that committee if I tried,
so I just aim to build up an overall effect
of Irish, Jewish, black, brown, and who-knows-
what-else union organizers and dangerous
communist sympathizers,
all poking their noses
into the respectable
white jury members'
private business.

When that police lieutenant testified
about the way Indians from Alaska to South America
all walked across an ancient land bridge from Asia,
it was easy to quote him describing Aztecs
as wildcats that must be caged, making them sound
like the enemy in our modern war—
Mexicans, Japanese—the average newspaper reader
doesn't know any difference, so human
sacrifice, living hearts carved from
Aztec-and-Asian savagery, that's a phrase
I plan to sprinkle all over the front page,
just to keep people wondering who will be
the next victim.

Now all I have to do is show
that across the border from Texas,
Mexican gangsters are probably
making deals with Nazi agents,
then sneaking
back here,
ready to pounce
on innocents.
Yeah, that's it, I need to create
a feeling of slinking submarines
as they glide underwater
to attack our ships.

Nothing sells newspapers as quickly
as fear.

Released
Lorena

I feel like two people at the same time,
one glad to be freed from jail, the other still
locked up
confused
frightened
angry.

¡Me pongo tan brava!
I become so outraged,
just as furious
as a brave but trapped
fighting
bull.

Life Sentences
Marisela

Girls and little kids like Ray
were all released before the trial,
but now we'll have to walk around
for the rest of our lives,
constantly REMEMBERING
how it FEELS
to be roughly CAPTURED
and falsely
ACCUSED!

There's no way out of the mess
except a lively jitterbug
to SHAKE away
all this sadness
with JAZZ!

Fantasía
Lorena

While Marisela goes back to her dance life,
I stay home, looking at comic books.

DARK SIDE OF TOWN was the worst headline,
with words that made the rest of this city feel
like white people had received official
permission
to fear
and hate
all of us.

No more newspapers for me.
Wonder Woman; Sheena, Queen of the Jungle;
Miss Fury—these are the lives
I want to see . . .
but with so many new female superheroes,
why do I still feel
totally
powerless?

Lawbreaker

Ray

Out of jail.
Right back to school.
Looking like a fool.
No GIANT drape.
No BIG dancing pants.
Just my ordinary shape.
Dressed like a gardener.
I look like old Papá.

Auto shop, woodshop, metal,
those teachers don't even expect me to
graduate.

Zoot suits might be illegal soon.
The Los Angeles City Council will vote.
Do they really expect to outlaw
all that JAZZ
and HAPPINESS?

When the remedial English teacher
asks me to translate my angrily muttered
words that she overhears,
I tell her ¡órale! I mean ¡ándale! go on,

¡épale!
you can
do it, *carnal* . . .
but I can't really explain this last word,
blood brother, cousin, kin?

She says I'm defining slang words
that don't really exist in English,
just by adding more of the same,
so I try: Wow!
Go get 'em!
Knock 'em dead,
pal!

Then she says I'm belligerent
and trying to fight, so I end up
in detention
AS USUAL.

Concerts
Manolito

No drapes in L.A.?
I've traveled to lots of places,
just like Cab Calloway in his glad rags,
bright-colored eastern zoot suits instead of these
West Coast sharkskin black or charcoal
pinstripes.

Real zooters don't need the right clothes
to dance; we just jump up on tabletops anyway!
Girls ride on shoulders, slide under boys' legs,
then get tossed up, flipped over, leap back up,
spin around, fly, swoop down, rise
and soar!

For boys, it's all about making the girls
look like acrobatic experts.
As long as we keep sharing this rhythm
of living, everyone feels like survivors
in wartime, 'cause that's what we are—alive!

Playing for zooters
who won't be allowed to wear baggy suits?
It would be a first for me, but this is Hollywood, movie land,

the glitzy world of the Palomar,
the same club where Benny Goodman himself
introduced the whole world to SWING music
on a hot summer night
way back in 1935.

Duke Ellington, Count Basie, Artie Shaw, Glenn Miller,
the jazz greats of every race have played here
and at the Orpheum
and the Million Dollar Theatre. . . .

All any teenage kid has to do is take a Red Line
streetcar toward downtown, then lie about age
and dance until dawn.

Black, Jewish, *mexicano*, Chinese,
this mixed-together dancing is the real reason
those old-fashioned white cops
hate, hate, hate
zoot suits.

They can't stand seeing
musicians as dark as I am,

not even while these brown kids'
brave older brothers
are overseas,
fighting and dying
in segregated
brigades.

Floating Upward
The Spirit of José Díaz Speaks

Change is a wind   *whoosh*
my life   as a ghost   was brief
and now   no one will ever be sure
who murdered me   even I
didn't see   all the faces
and knife blades

but change is a wind   *whoosh*   my life
from the day I was given to the light   by Mamá
in Durango, México   to the night when I was taken
from this world   on a breeze of frog song   and bird eyes

all those years   following crops   lettuce in Salinas,
tasty grapes in Parlier, then the sweet oranges of Pomona,
and dry white cotton in Firebaugh, plump purple plums
in Santa Clara, and now here, my chance   to join
the U.S. Army   and prove   my loyalty
gone
      like bird flight
              sunlight
                     space. . . .

BAREFOOT

May 1943

Our Shrinking World
Lorena

No letters from Nico.
How long has it been
since I thought of my older brother
by his little-boy-playing-outside
nickname?

Shortages at home—rationed sugar,
not to mention rubber and gasoline
for anyone lucky enough to own a car.

Factories switch
from making jukeboxes to weapons,
and from sewing dresses to stitching
lifesaving parachutes.

Even the dances are quieter, with so many
of the best musicians signing up to fight, trading
sweet melodies
for rattling
machine guns.

Knife
Marisela

Daydreaming about a handsome jazz musician
just gets me in TROUBLE, when fantasies
about romance should bring joy, not confusion.

Ay Dios, too fast, oh God, *tan rápido*
while my mind races, until once again
I'm ordered to SLOW down, chop LESS,
leave some fresh green spinach
for the other girls, so men can cook it
down to a slimy mess, stuff it into cans,
and sell it, calling the soggy leaves
healthy.

Keeping men in uniforms sturdy, that's what
this spinach craze is all about, cartoons
and comic strips about Popeye the Sailor Man,
who gobbles green magic to make himself
STRONG.

Lorena, with her quiet STRENGTH,
says all we really need to think about
is JUSTICE, fairness, a world
where we could be paid
the SAME as men,

get hired for BETTER jobs,
and make enough to save
tuition
for school.

Lorena says she wants to be
a secretary, but I think if she keeps
talking like that, she'll end up being
la jefa,
the BOSS!

A Future?
Lorena

There must be some way to pay for
secretarial school, typing lessons,
shorthand, dictation, filing, answering
telephones the way businessmen expect,
in swift,
perfect English
with no accent at all,
not even the occasional
¡Ay Dios!
to plead for help
from a shared God
who surely must
understand
every
language.

Dancing at the All Nations Club
Marisela

Ray assures me that it's okay
to dance with anyone of any race,
even off-duty musicians,
dark or light.

So I learn new steps from back east,
bailando con el cubano who wears
suits as bright as a sunny sky,
gold or turquoise, depending
on the music, wild big band
or casual jam session, either way
I practice FLYING as I LEAP
over his shoulders,
slide low beneath him, then RISE UP
                    feeling weightless
and FREE,
even though this is a church club
with stern old ladies watching, little kids giggling,
and every once in a while, my bored sister
sighing, *Ay Dios.*

What would the nosy crowd say if they knew
that I'm interested in more than just dancing . . . ?

City Life
Ray

If you can't dance
with your neighbors,
you live in the wrong
place.

¡Ritmo!
Manolito

Back on the island
I played congas and bongós,
but now in this traveling big band,
I focus on kettle drums and cymbals,
metallic, not wood and goatskin
rumbling and tapping so naturally
against my hands, fingers and palms
transformed into sound waves. . . .

When white sailors call me Snow,
I tell them to use
my name—but I can see
that some who come
from southern states
seem to really think
I'm being too bold for a dark foreigner,
so I play faster to trip their steps,
and I dance closer when *la mexicana*
chooses me after my shift ends and another
island drummer takes my place playing *el ritmo*,
the *afrocubano* rhythm that makes people
of any color

fly
slide
spin!

Dancing doesn't seem like a quiet enough way
to really get to know someone, but we find
plenty of chances
to talk
hold hands
ask questions
whisper answers. . . .

Front-Page News
Reporter #1

After the Sleepy Lagoon trial dragged on
and sentences were finally declared, a bunch
of Mexican kids went to San Quentin for life.

Now overseas battles fill every page,
so I dream up a new angle, and even though
it makes me feel old-fashioned, it's the law,
so I use it, reminding my readers that the California
Civil Code of 1941 states very clearly: "All marriages
of white persons with Negroes, Mongolians, members
of the Malay race, or mulattoes are illegal
and void."

No intermarriage is allowed,
so why weren't Mexicans
included?
It's a detail overlooked
by the law, one that means
las señoritas de la USO
can marry white sailors,
but they can't marry blacks,
so all this scandalous
interracial

jazz dancing
might sooner or later
lead to CRIMES OF THE HEART,
a passionate headline
with a bittersweet
echoing sound
that makes
lonely housewives
pay attention
to my articles.

I imagine the sailors
and police
notice too.

After fear, my next-best seller
is anger.

After the Imaginary Great Air Raid
Reporter #2

Last year's Japanese invasion of Los Angeles
never happened, but predicting that it would
helped us sell plenty of newspapers,
and now this interracial dancing
angle
might be almost
as profitable.

Why wait for real-life drama
when I can just go ahead
and speculate?

Helping Abuela in the Backyard
Ray

With zoot suits dangerously illegal, my parents
make me stay home and scrub laundry
in a shed, or hoe weeds in the victory garden,
eggplant, jicama, okra, tomatoes,
jalapeños, cilantro, squash,
it's amazing how many flavors
can be angrily yanked from the earth
when my grandma uses my muscles
and her faith in the generosity
of dirt.

Rice, potatoes, flour, pinto beans,
I'm sent to the store to fetch big cloth
sacos filled with food, then I help Abuela
bleach the sacks—girls' work,
so I absolutely refuse
to have anything to do
with stitching bean sack clothing
or embroidering flowery
designs.

Memorias
Abuela

I remember long ago
when I was young enough
to climb a pepper tree at home
in México,
or play
at making snails race,
then run, run, run away
when the soldiers
of Pancho Villa
came.

¿Cómo es posible que una vida—one life
can hold
both the revolution
of 1910 in my birth *tierra*
and this worldwide *guerra* now,
with my oldest grandson gone
and the young one always
in trouble?

Patches of Time
Ray

Tierra. Earth.
Guerra. War.
So many rhymes
inside my grandma's
tired old mind.

It's easy to watch her twirl a polka,
then show her my own
modern moves.

Together we laugh
as she tries to imitate
my COOL new way
of inventing
a HOPPING jitterbug
garden-crossing step.

By the time we're finished, it's hard to say
whether we're dancing through her youth
or mine.

The Month of Flowers
Lorena

Voladas, our grandma calls us, flown girls,
carried away by a wind
of wildness.

So we quiet down as we obediently agree
to carry flowers to the altar of María
each evening in May, marching in a long
procession of girls and women, all of us
dressed in white, our heads covered
with lacy veils, as we deliver armloads
of homegrown roses, *el ofrecimiento*,
an offering and a plea
for the safety
of soldiers,
our brother
overseas.

Las voladas
Marisela

Las voladas is a criticism
meaning "flown-away girls,"
but I love the soaring SOUND!
If only I really could FLY up high and FAR away
from the painful SIGHT
of gold stars in windows,
each one in honor of a father, son,
or brother
lost
FOREVER.

Inside each of those grieving homes
there's a funeral flag, folded
and treasured,
all the stars
of the U.S.
sparkling
with SORROW.

Sneaking OUT
Ray

I know I'm not supposed to wear my cool suit,
but I'm a ZOOT cat, hip cat, Lindy Hopping *vato* LOCO,
so I won't let anyone tell me how to dress
or when to go out dancing, *sí, simón*, I slip away
no matter how often Papá warns me,
and even when Mami tries
to make me feel guilty
by praying for the safety
of Nicolás,
I still climb
over the windowsill
at midnight
when everyone else
is sleeping.

I wear a black hat
to cover up my ducktail hair,
and shoe soles that I made myself,
building them up high
with old tire rubber,
just like *huarache* sandals
from Tijuana,
so they'll
last longer

and save leather,
helping the war effort—but also
a double-thick sole works like an anchor,
making me strong
when I lift a girl
UP
over my head,
swing her HIGH,
make her FLY,
turning both of us
into dance contest
SUPER-heroes!

Robbed
Ray

Policemen are supposed to protect people.
Instead they yell, spin me around,
order me to take off my shoes
then my socks
    naked feet
      exposed heart
       all my feelings
         so OPENLY displayed
          on the surface
           of my face.

When they toss my shoes and socks
into their car, I RACE away, barefoot
on the spit-stained
    ugliness
      of sidewalks,
        strangers laughing
        STRANGELY.

Did You See That Dark Kid?
Sailor #1

Cops sent him home barefoot.
They even made him take off his socks!
Deadly weapons, that's what those foreign shoes are,
the homemade ones with thick rubber soles
that must weigh as much
as a brick.

City life is so lively that the sight
of a shoeless Spanish boy makes me laugh
even louder and longer than that newspaper cartoon
about Zoot Suit Yokum, the stupidest guy
in the world, a not-super-hero so dumb
that all us navy recruits argue
about who gets to read
the Sunday funny section
first.

It's always me.
I win because I've got the most muscular
attitude in the world.

Feeling Like a Bully
Sailor #2

I don't like the way laughing
at that barefoot kid made me feel,
but still, Zoot Suit Yokum is so silly
and foolish
that I tell myself
we're just having
a bit of fun in this big, wild city
before heading out to kill
or be
killed.

Any teen in a big suit must know
that he's taking the risk of being
stripped down to ridiculous
naked
feet.

Barefoot?
Mami

¿Sin zapatos?
¡Ay, no!

Dios, protect Nicolás from *los* Nazis
and Ray from *la policía* right here
in our own
city.

Imagínate, God, how it feels for a mother
to work hard, hard, hard
just so her children
never have to run
shoeless
like I did
when I was little, so many sharp
rocks, shells, and broken bottles
hidden in beach sand,
slicing
my bare toes.

City Life or Countryside?

Papá

The work was a lot harder
when we followed crops,
moving every season,
never feeling settled,
no chance for our children
to stay in school.

Now Ray is the only one still studying,
I couldn't keep the girls from dropping out,
but look at him, beaten up, barefoot, ashamed,
maybe he'd be better off if we'd stayed
out on the road, Lost Hills for cotton,
Sanger in peach season,
no place to dance
in fancy clothes
that pull like a magnet,
attracting attention,
policía,
trouble.

June Gloom Comes Early
Lorena

Fog is on its way.
There will be no work.
The lag between seasons
so endless
once spinach is over,
and peaches
won't start
until *agosto*
swimming season
August heat
crazy
loco.

So I work with Abuela
in her quiet little victory garden,
where she tends fruit trees
and vegetables,
all these patches of hot *chiles*
so spicy
that red heat
scalds my fingertips
just as brightly
as any cooking flame.

Food grown at home
means less bought in stores,
leaving plenty
for the army,
navy,
marines.

All Marisela ever talks about
is her favorite *cubano* musician,
the one she calls Manolito, showing
that she knows him, and maybe they've
already crossed the line way past friendship,
but Ray likes to speculate—which
military branch
will he choose
when he's old enough
to fight and die for
our country.

I agree that marines have
the most attractive uniforms,
but there's something to be said
for the air force, warplanes
soaring high above our heads
on their way
to wherever Nico
might be wishing

to be rescued,
or waiting
to be
buried.

MIA.
Missing in action.
It's a gloomy,
pre-June telegram
that sends all of us
on a pilgrimage
to an altar
on a hilltop.

While the rest of us walk slowly,
our bodies and minds weighed down by horror,
Abuela travels on her knees, letting the road's
rough gravel
scrape her skin,
a plea
made of flesh,
her prayer
a trail
of raw,
bleeding
hope.

PEELED

June 1943

Fear
Ray

MIA means "missing in action,"
but in Spanish it also means *mía*,
"mine, belonging to me,"
like that day last month when I walked
on my own two straight *piernas*, my legs,
while Abuela shuffled painfully along
on her bent, bleeding knees.
I felt so useless and selfish,
just a little kid who can't fight beside
my brother, or search when he
goes missing.

I know the prayers
flowers
altars
make my grandma feel dream-filled
and hopeful,
but I need a plea
that I can experience in my bones,
not just words in my mind,
so I DANCE
all alone
each night
at home

while everyone else
is asleep
and only God
sees me
furiously
leaping. . . .

Mind in the AIR
heart on the ground
my silent
prayer
for Nico
RISES
and floats.

Divided
Marisela

My dreams and heart
are spinning all over
a daydreamed
moonlit
dance floor
with MANOLITO . . .

but the rest of me
stays close to Abuela
and my mother,
helping them pray
for my missing
brother.

Nonsense

Lorena

A few nights after the procession
to that hilltop altar of Santa María,
we danced at the Aragon Ballroom
on the Venice pier, until sailors
got drunk and chased Ray
onto the beach,
then the boardwalk,
a crowded trail
of chaos
that suddenly turned
into a fight . . .

but my little brother
wasn't the only kid
kicking and punching,
even though he was one
of the few
arrested.

How can something
as simple
and ordinary
as a jitterbug
get so twisted,

like a vine
on a fence,
tendrils
of fear
twining
high
as we
desperately
try
to grasp
calm
common
sense?

Vision

Ray

All I did was defend my sisters
against wolf-whistling *brutos*.

I wasn't even wearing my cool
zoot drapes.

But cops always see me
as an invading foreigner
who walks and talks
with too much
CONFIDENCE.

Being a citizen born in the U.S. is never
enough protection, so from now on
maybe I'll think of myself
as a wanderer,
not shut out
or locked in
but separate and FREE.

Punished
Marisela

Radio newsmen call us wild.
Printed headlines make us sound even worse,
using words like *immoral, dangerous, vile.*
Everyone talks like we're the ones who are SCARY!

All Lorena and I did was DANCE,
and Ray just fought back
when he was ATTACKED.

Ay, how beautifully I tried to fly above the floor,
and now I'm scolded by Mami and Papá,
who don't seem to believe in my innocence.

What if I'm not allowed to be a jazz owl anymore?
My sister and I still need to go out, work hard,
and bring home money, walking back late
with our chaperone, Ray,
who never stops risking his life
to escort us.

Maybe I really do need to be more cautious
like Lorena.

Ready for Anything
Reporter #1

Rowdy.
Riled up.
I choose my ominous *R* words carefully,
trying to describe rumbles of restlessness
in the ramshackle neighborhood
where Mexicans have been brooding
for a long time, angry because their shacks
were torn down to build that sturdy armory
for training new sailors and stockpiling
ferocious war weapons.

Now it's all finally turning into a real story!
Sailors scare local girls.
Zooters frighten navy wives.
A military man's car cuts in front
of local teens who are walking around
in their fancy suits, just waiting
to break beer bottles
and challenge authority.

Retaliation. Revenge.
When the inevitable turmoil
finally rises up, I'll be there,

ready to write
about
rage.

One word that I plan to repeat over and over
in this long article about dangerous influences
is *Afro-Cuban*, with respect to music,
because it sounds even more vicious
than Aztec warriors
demanding
a sacrifice.

Latin dance.
That's what the other reporters prefer.
Latin jazz.

Yeah, even older readers love the rhumba,
so they feel more comfortable with words
that make people think of tropical romance,
but comfort doesn't move newspapers.
Tribal warfare.
That's what sells.

How Can *la música* Be Dangerous?
Manolito

I'm young, but age isn't everything
when it comes to experience playing island drums
that claimed my rhythmic fingers
almost from birth.

I've been performing ever since
I was thirteen, on the road all over Cuba,
then México City, Chicago, New York, Paris,
free to choose my jobs
because all the best orchestra leaders
want islanders born with congas, bongós,
and rumba drums
in our hands
and on our minds.

It makes me furious when Americans pretend
to be Cuban just so they can sell jazz-craze
music—Alvino Rey is really Alvin McBurney,
Alfredo Méndez is Alfred Mendelsohn,
Don Carlos is Lou Gold, and Chico Bullo
used to call himself Chick Bullock—
but the truth is nothing annoys me more
than lazy pronunciation, in newspapers
where *rumba*

is spelled *rhumba*,
the *u* rhyming with *dull*
instead of
cool.

If I didn't have those sweet dance nights
with Marisela
to keep me from fleeing,
I'd be leaving L.A. right now,
headed for Memphis
or New Orleans.

No More Retorts
Reporter #1

Letters like that one from a foreign musician
should never again be printed
in the editorial section!

Who is he to say that I'm wrong
when I call it the "Spanish tinge"
instead of giving his people credit
for the syncopated four-beat rhythm
of Saint Louis blues?

I don't care if Machito and his Afro-Cuban orchestra
were the first ones to introduce a certain kind
of tropical jazz craze
in these United States.

All I care about is my readers,
and most of them like a tame rhumba,
not that crazy, impossible-to-copy,
wild island
rumba.

June 3, 1943
Reporter #2

While my competitor argues
about musical influences,
real news almost escapes
the attention
of dance fools.

History starts with a dim-out,
not even a blackout, just lights that fade
while sailors and zooters
meet and clash
on the shadowy corner
of Euclid and Whittier.

6:00 p.m.
Sixteen navy men rush from a bus
on Sunset Boulevard, then strut north on Figueroa
toward the armory, but first they have to pass
Alpine, a street where zooters
curse them.

Around the same time, two sailors
leave the armory,
prowling toward Adobe Street,

and get cussed out
by girls—one man even claims
that a rude *señorita*
gives him a Nazi salute,
mocking
his U.S. uniform
as she calls him
a bullying
brute.

Now the only question in my mind is
do I take the angle that makes her seem
Asian-eyed and foreign, like the enemy
in Japan, or do I let her lead me
into the risky quagmire of accusations
about Nazi-style racial hatred
on the part
of otherwise dignified
all-American
sailors?

That Same Night
Reporter #3

8:00 p.m.
Fifty sailors burst
toward downtown!

Hidden weapons—makeshift,
not military.

Broom handles, weight-lifting dumbbells,
hammers, rocks, belt buckles, and even
the rougher parts
of palm tree fronds,
plucked up off the street
because they're heavy enough
to do real harm,
with those saw-toothed edges
that are naturally
so sharp.

The mob of raging sailors goes boiling
along Figueroa
to Alpine,
followed by cars

packed with men
in uniform.

In a frenzy, they search for zooters,
but few can be found, because local kids
have been invited to a meeting with the police
to talk about forming a clubhouse, someplace
to keep teens off the streets, out of trouble—
a rec center where they can play basketball
or baseball. . . .

With no Mexican kids to beat up,
the military men just keep
roaming
hunting
like packs
of predators. . . .

Vicious
Ray

I didn't go to that police rec center meeting
because I was doing what I always do, obediently
chaperoning my sisters.

Mostly we're expected to stay safely at home,
except for my school and the owl sisters' work,
but sometimes we stop along the way
to watch a movie at the Carmen Theater,
which seems so tame
compared with the wildness
of dance halls.

So while Marisela and Lorena are busy laughing
at cartoons, armed sailors barge in, switch on
the lights,
scout the aisles,
and choose me, grab me, drag me outside. . . .

The rest is a blur of fists, boots, baseball bats,
bruises, blood, and noise—my sisters'
terrified
SHRIEKS.

I used to spend my energy
trying to avoid getting beaten up
by guys from other neighborhoods.

I never imagined the worst BLOWS
to my JAW
CHEEK
CHEST
HEART
would come from strangers
who are just passing through **MY** city
on their way to faraway battles.

It's useless trying to fight back
against so many; all I can do is curl
into a ball, protecting my head
with cupped hands, feeling
as helpless
as a turtle
on its back. . . .

Smoke
Lorena

Violence beyond belief.
Hatred without any explanation.
Stripped, all of them, boys even younger
than Ray, mere children, their clothes torn off,
slashed, piled in the aisles, and set aflame,
the dark cloth of wide zoot suits
burning,
barbaric
unimaginable
brutality
yet real,
so hideous,
this truth
la verdad.

I always thought girls were the only ones
who needed to be careful, but this is an attack
against boys, the same sailors we danced with
now trying to kill
my little brother.

Horrified
Marisela

Lying on the street in his white underwear,
poor Ray, unconscious and bleeding,
looks as fragile
as a baby bird.

Lorena and I rush to help him, but the sailors
are still so dangerous, GLARING at us
and rolling those HARD weapons
around in their hands, the baseball bats
just as terrifying
as gun barrels.

Why don't the police
put a stop to this OUTRAGE?

Ay Dios, the horror just goes on
and on. . . .

What about Manolito, where is he?
Oh, please, God, let him be SAFE. . . .

Knowing
Lorena

Suddenly I understand all the girls
who've been *zooterinas*
for so long,
dressed like rebels
to show that women
are strong.

Now, with Ray motionless and bleeding
right in front of me, and the sailors still acting
insane as they grab kids and hurl them
off streetcars
onto the pavement,
beating, stripping, humiliating boys
in front of us—sisters, girlfriends,
even mothers. . . .

Now, with all this madness raging around me,
I'm not calm or sensible.
I crave revenge,
knowing how desperate it feels to need
justice.

A Mess
Policeman #1

We haul broken-bone boys
from the movie theater
and streetcars
to that hospital
on Georgia Street.

No point arresting sailors,
even though they're really acting crazy.

The penalty for military men who riot is death,
so why stir up complicated troubles
in wartime?

Our men in uniform deserve respect.
Don't they?

I sure don't want to be the first
law enforcement officer
photographed
handcuffing
a hero.

Mob Violence
Policeman #2

June 4.
Sailors plunge deep into East L.A.
This time they go after entire Mexican neighborhoods,
ordering twenty yellow cabs, then paying the taxi drivers
to carry them all the way to Boyle Heights,
where they attack cafés, restaurants, and theaters,
stripping the clothes off teenage boys, burning zoot suits,
until hysteria spreads
and grows like wildfire,
attracting soldiers and marines
all the way from San Diego to El Toro. . . .

It's a real riot now, huge and out of control,
so we do the only thing we can think of,
rounding up the kids for their own protection.

I don't know a single cop willing to arrest
military men in uniform.

Maybe it's not fair, but hey, sometimes we
lose our tempers too.

June 5
Manolito

Main Street and 3rd.
The Aztec Recording Company.
A chance to make music, but I'm
the only one in a zoot suit. All the others
are composers, writers, and singers
from Texas and México, dressed
in street clothes.

When I spot sailors marching
arm in arm, like a horde of swarming
hornets, I guess what's coming. It's easy to imagine
how I'll be viewed—*negro*, black, not just *cubano*
or a foreigner, definitely not just a musician.
Hunted.
That's how it feels.
These men who danced to my drums
a few days ago, they're predators now, prowling,
so eager to kill me. . . .

All I can do is run, trying to stay alive
in a hate-crazed time.

June 6
Ray

Those *pinches locos* didn't actually set ME on fire
but my shape
contained inside my burning clothes
went up in **FLAMES**.

So now, in the hospital, I feel FORMLESS,
trying to figure out
how to make my arms
and legs
move
when they feel like wisps
of shrinking smoke.

Humiliation—it's a SILENCE, not a sound.
Even with two languages, *dos idiomas*,
I can think of only one word to describe
this RAGE and **SHAME**.

Pelado. Peeled.
Those are the only scorched syllables
my tormented mind
can FIND.

The sailors might as well have sliced off
my SKIN
and set the FLESH
underneath
on **FIRE**.

Torture, that's what this is,
the kind of treatment
no one's ever supposed to suffer
in real life, only in horror movies
and nightmares.

June 7
Sailor #1

Tonight we'll strike
every dark-skinned part of this city.

We've got civilians joining now,
enough men to swoop all over East L.A.
and Watts
at the same time. . . .

Mexicans, blacks—back home
in the South, I was taught to think of them
all
as the same
thing.

Dangerous.
That's how I feel!
This fight will be good practice
for real
foreign
battlefields.

Listening to Teens

Reporter #1

They're beating up colored kids in Watts now
along with the Mexicans.

Reporter #2

It's a story, all right—that intellectual editor
of a small local paper
has organized a meeting of teenagers,
asking the East L.A. boys to make peace.
No revenge.
No retaliation.

Reporter #3

"Isn't this a free country?" one kid asks
at the meeting. "Can't we wear the kind of clothes
that we like?" I find it both newsworthy
and sad
that he still thinks
this is about
suits
instead of skin.

12th and Central
Ray

Two hundred boys agree to go home
after the meeting.
Not me.
¡Órale!

Fifty of us head downtown to PROTECT
the people who live there.
Most of the guys wear drapes, but mine
are ashes
because this is hell,
el infierno,
that's what I
SEE.

Sailors, soldiers, civilians,
all **stripping** and **beating up MY friends**
while cops arrest **US**, not **them**.

I'll never forget.
No, not me.

For Their Own Protection

Policeman #1

Belts and boots bash faces.
Blood on the sidewalk.
Mothers trying to defend
teenage sons.

How was I supposed to know
there was a woman with a baby
right behind me?

I spun around in a circle and slammed
any face
I could find
with my nightstick.

Policeman #2

Reporters everywhere.
Cameras.
But we have our orders:
Arrest Mexican kids, not sailors, soldiers,
or U.S. Marines.

Policeman #3

Where's the shore patrol?
Why hasn't the navy shut those gates
at the armory?

How can the United States military
keep letting drunk recruits run wild,
ruining
this whole city?

11:30 p.m.

Sailor #1

Stripping a kid makes him look so small.
Lighting this match to burn zoot suits
makes me think of my bold granddaddy,
back in his good old KKK days, setting fires
on front lawns.

Sailor #2

Jazz dancing
race mixing
blues music
burn!

Sailor #3

I don't know how I feel about any of this,
but I'll figure it out tomorrow, because right now
all I need to do is fit in with this crowd, the mob.
As soon as we ship out overseas to the real war,
my life
will depend
on this crazy blaze
of brotherly bonds and memories, friendship.
Won't it?

June 8
Mami

Last night I leaned
over the fence
and spat
in a rude
sailor's face.

¡Bruto! I called him.
How dare he think of himself
as powerful and brave, when my firstborn,
Nicolás,
is the real
hero?

June 8
Lorena

Finally an official crackdown, ending
the worst of the violence. . . .

Shore leave has been canceled,
and Los Angeles is off-limits to all branches
of the military, even the coast guard.

Radio reporters keep saying "Zoot Suit Riots,"
but what happened here was military, not
civilian.

Why don't they use the right words
and admit that local teens weren't the ones
who went completely
insane?

Everyone needs to start saying
Sailor Riots, instead of blaming
boys like Ray.

June 8
Marisela

Will anyone EVER dance again?
How will I find Manolito *el músico*?
Is there life beyond this time of never-ending
uncertainty?

¡One of the most reassuring things about Spanish
is the way every thought can be SEEN in advance,
foretold by an upside-down exclamation
or question mark!

¿Will today once again
be a waking NIGHTMARE
of violent
SAILOR RIOTS?

¿What about TOMORROW?
¿Can this CRAZY city ever
feel SAFE?

June 8
Papá

Nearly a hundred kids were arrested
and only two servicemen.

Blowing off steam, that's the way politicians
are defending the sailors' actions, in all those
pointless newspaper interviews
and on *la radio*.

One of them even quotes an Army Flying School
pilot trainee who describes his part in the riots
as "cleaning up L.A."

¡En mi opinión, it was poison that seeped
from places where people still think
the Civil War
never ended!

¡Watcha!
Ray

I blame those cops who SEIZED my SHOES.
They set the hateful example, started that ugly
pattern,
showed me that I'm not seen
as HUMAN in their eyes.

Sailors were watching; they saw how easily
a kid like me could be defeated, just by the
NAKEDNESS
of FEET.

Pos, I promise it won't happen again.
From now on I'll ALWAYS
be armed
with caution.

Back to Work
Lorena

Eleanor Roosevelt, the president's wife,
called it a race riot, so now city officials say,
"That's not true, we like Mexicans, just look
how we go to Olvera Street to eat tacos
and wear big ranchero hats, listening
to mariachi music, so lively
and cheerful."

Well, I feel like our brains are being used as piñatas,
with everyone trying to break open my thoughts
so they can understand *mexicanos*, but by now
they should know me.
I'm the one
who makes it possible
for sailors and soldiers to eat
overseas,
where all they have
is the food
we slice
pack
and seal
into hard

round
metal
cans.

Each bite of anything
that contains
tomato sauce
spinach
or peaches
should taste
so bitter and salty
after being wildly spiced
with my fears
and
tears.

I don't know what I can do to change anything,
but there must be some way to grow
like one of Abuela's garden plants,
changing directions to find
sunlight.

Dancing Again
Marisela

Returning to work feels as strange as traveling
through time, trying to reach last week, before
all that VIOLENCE changed
everything. . . .

But at least Ray SURVIVED,
and Manolito, too, the best jitterbug partner
who ever helped me
          break free
from gravity
                        to leap
                  twirl
                                    SOAR

and land
      safely!

If he asked me to marry him right now,
I'd shout
YES!

Locos
Manolito

Crazy, both of us.
Yes, it's true, we're *locos*,
because everyone knows
un cubano negro
can't marry
a brown *mexicana*,
not here in Los Angeles,
where the law turns her
into a white girl,
even though sailors, policemen,
and reporters
treat her family like enemy
invaders.

So I'll go out on the road,
but I'll come back again
someday soon, when we're a bit older
and this hate-crazed city
regains
its sanity.

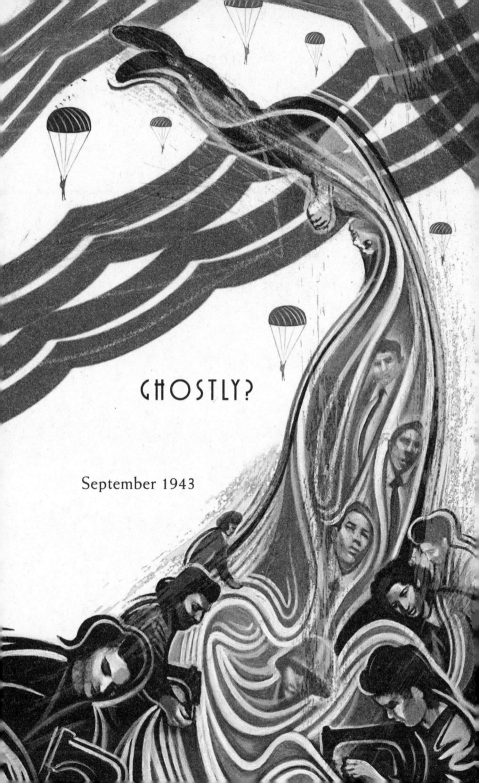

GHOSTLY?

September 1943

Awareness
Ray

Swimming season passes without a single
submerged stroke, because my temper
feels too hot to be cooled
by water.

Is the spirit of José Díaz homeless,
still soaring above Sleepy Lagoon?

Or is he winged,
angelic,
blessed?

Can he see far beyond
this haunted
imitation
of life?

How can I ever feel normal/*normal*
on streets where my body was stripped,
my mind peeled, turning me into **El Pelado**.
If so many others hadn't experienced
the same rage, that could be my new
nickname instead of Sombra/Shadow,

a living,
shifting,
floating
ghost.

We all have many names now, my friends
who understand one another, this group
made up of an entire neighborhood,
los carnales, the kinfolk I choose
because it's so much easier
to understand
tangled memories
than shared birth. . . .

So each time I dance now, the steps
are my own, a *pachuco* hop, not the Lindy,
my new black zoot suit, bought with borrowed
money, daring those crazy sailors
to rage again—just let them try,
because this time
we'll WIN.

Cannery Blues
Marisela

With the Sailor Riots already fading
into a troubling vagueness of memories,
los duraznos shed peach fuzz all over
my boring clothes, so I'm surprised
to find myself wishing
for more work,
not less.

I need to stay busy, or I'll go crazy with longing!
There's no point dressing nicely, when Mami and Papá
won't let me stay out late anymore, only allowing us
to work day shifts, even though refusing
odd hours
puts me and Lorena at risk
for getting fired.

My worst fear isn't more violence.
It's never seeing Manolito
again.

Growing
Lorena

Sorrowful
danceless
joyless
both of us
are girls
who move
like gazelles
inside our tiny
zoo cage of limitations,
unable to slide
leap
glide
except within
our ever-increasingly wide
imaginations.

I can see Marisela's new strength
as clearly as if it were built
of bricks.

This Slow Life
Marisela

Time SAGGED
    as soon as he left.

I receive letters and postcards
    from all over México, where he claims
that *la música cubana* is almost as popular
    as *mexicano* movies are in his island
homeland.

Different accents.
    Unique rhythms.
Each country of Latin America
    sounds so special
the way he describes them.
    How will I EVER be able to travel
with his band
    when I can't even go to the
All Nations Church
dance club?

Thinking of all the words we enjoyed comparing,
I remember the way he said *lechuza*
instead of *tecolote*

when he called me a night owl,
and *mondongo* instead of *menudo*
when we shared a bowl of tripe soup,
maní in place of *cacahuate*
as a name for roasted peanuts,
fruta bomba, not papaya,
and *pavo* instead of *guajolote*
for a turkey on Thanksgiving. . . .

To Manolito, the word *tortilla*
meant "omelet," and a bus was *la guagua*,
a *campesino*, farmworker, *un guajiro*. . . .

The one thing we agreed on was that *el español*
is NOT a foreign language in California, because
it was spoken here long before *el inglés*
invaded.

So we found it easy to follow the habit
of letting SWEET words mix and roll like a river
tumbling toward a waterfall
of meanings.

Decisions
Lorena

Union organizers
prowl near the cannery.

We're warned by checkers
to keep our distance . . .
but Marisela and I finally know
our own minds.

Yes, we're tired of taking orders
from narrow-brained men who don't care
about my brother or my father, or the way
we've worked here for so long but still
can't qualify for men's jobs, men's pay,
respect.

Papá decided that he isn't old enough
to stay out of the war anymore, so he just
signed up and shipped out,
hoping to find some clue
to the disappearance
of Nicolás.

Now my sister and I stand up boldly
singing
at a secret meeting,
agreeing that it's time
for the unity
of a union.

If we can't receive
the same hourly wage as a man,
at least we can display our own
female
courage.

Organizing My Own Voice
Marisela

Manolito used to say that jazz
grew from SADNESS, a desperate need
to invite dance moves
into our hearts,
one wildly
hopeful rhythm
at a time, like musical
birds in a forest
creating a territory marked
by natural melodies
and wingbeats.

So when I finally have a chance
to speak my mind at a union meeting,
I say EXACTLY what I'm thinking
in the form
of a PROTEST song.

Lorena wrote the strong words,
but I'm the one who SINGS so
powerfully!

Our Demands

Lorena

We need dry floors
so we won't slip
on peach juice,
and gloves and goggles
in hot pepper season
to keep our fingers and eyes
from burning so fiercely
that flesh turns to blisters
and vision
is blurred.

Women like Mami, at walnut packing plants,
should never lose their hammers as a punishment
for cracking hard shells too rapidly
in an effort to make more money
for their families—no, it's not right,
forcing her to crush nuts
with bare knuckles,
bruised,
bleeding.

A Growing Chorus
Marisela

Safe, healthy working conditions.
THAT'S ALL WE ASK IN OUR HEARTFELT
SONG.

The rhythm
is traditional.
The song is
told in the form
of a ballad,
a STORY,
un corrido,
not jazz.

Soon even the older women join in,
SINGING of *ESPERANZA*/HOPE
for EQUALITY!

It's Not Enough

Lorena

Safe conditions are important,
but I want more, so much more,
I need
dignidad.
Dignity.

Yes/*sí*, I demand my bilingual freedom/*libertad*
to speak openly, without fear of getting fired
for being a troublemaker.

In my *opinión*, the real trouble is made
by people who don't listen
to our song,
our story.

Living Dangerously
Marisela

Some of the union songs at meetings
teach HISTORY.

1903
Mexican and Japanese farmworkers
joined together in Oxnard, SUCCEEDING
because their strike was UNIFIED.
That's what the word *unión*
means.

1920s
More walkouts, but farmers never
took the refusal to work seriously, until:

1930s
Agricultural strikes ALL OVER California.
Mexican Americans, Filipinos, and dust-bowl
refugees from Oklahoma and Arkansas
ALL WORKED TOGETHER, demanding
better wages—unity, that's what
helped them, even though
some were deported
or beaten,
even KILLED.

When *The Grapes of Wrath*
was being filmed, the Motion Picture Guild
showed up in Shafter, a little town near Bakersfield,
to throw a party with food and praise
for ten thousand migrant
farmworkers.

I could read that book to find out
what people are talking about when they say
that John Steinbeck
learned from US.

Pamphlets.
Mimeograph machines.
I could learn it ALL, how to SPEAK UP
on paper, translating into many
languages, so that every woman
at this cannery knows how to ask
for fair treatment.

I could be just as calm and sensible
as my sister, without losing my own eager
ENERGY!

By the time I've painted my first poster
asking everyone to donate blood to the Red Cross
as proof of patriotic loyalty, I feel so USEFUL
that I almost forget what it felt like to have
un novio,
a boyfriend—
Manolito,
my heart's
true partner.

These days only my fingers
know how to
DANCE
on paper.

What Will the Future Be Like?

Lorena

While peach season leads to tomatoes,
Marisela is gradually transformed
from one person into another,
without losing her original
self.

I'm changing
too, my hair bobbed short,
my clothes so deliberately dull
that no one would dream of wearing them
to a dance.

I spend part of my paycheck on union dues
for dignity
and part on war bonds to help Papá and Nico
fight for liberty
from the Nazis' hateful ways . . .
but who will struggle for freedom from racial hatred
here
at home?

Scarred
Ray

None of those boys who were
PEELED
during the Sailor Riots
will ever be able to forget
how we
vanished.

When your clothes are STRIPPED AWAY
by raging strangers, something invisible
happens inside your rib cage.
¡Corazón!
Heart!
That's what I exposed
by SURVIVING.

So now when I fight, each PUNCH
is like a dance move, natural
and strategically planned,
all at the same rhythmic *TIEMPO/TIME*.

Expelled from School
Ray

Kicked out.
Busted.
Booted.
Defeated.
Too many battles
with other angry guys,
carnales—brotherlike neighbors
who got peeled
and ended up
scarred
scared
lonely
just
like
me.

Swing Shift
Lorena

Deciding to leave the cannery is easy.
One of our neighbors helps me apply
to a parachute factory so far out in the desert
that we have to share the price of an old car
and take turns learning to drive,
instead of relying on buses
and streetcars.

Sewing is a skill all the girls know,
taught by our grandmothers when we were little.
My stitches are perfect, the parachute cloth
so fiercely strong that I feel certain
this sharp needle and sturdy thread
will save lives,
maybe my own.

Yes, why shouldn't women
learn to fly, just like men?

We sit in a circle, female workers
from so many places, dark and light
together.

Some were born in Mississippi,
others are refugees from Armenia, Russia,
Poland, but there aren't any language barriers
when we dream
of seeing
our parachutes
on newsreels,
unfolding over
the grateful
smiles
of rescued
pilots.

Signs
Lorena

On the long daily drive all the way
from East L.A. to Lancaster, I glance up
at new billboards
that speak to me
in Spanish:
AMERICANOS TODOS.
LUCHAMOS POR LA VICTORIA.
ESTA GUERRA ES SUYA.
AMERICANS ALL.
WE FIGHT FOR VICTORY.
THIS WAR IS YOURS.

The Office of War Information
and the Office of the Coordinator
of Inter-American Affairs
have decided to invite
people like me
to apply for jobs
in aircraft factories. . . .

So I could actually be
a little bit closer to my new dream
of learning to be a pilot

in a world where men
can't imagine
women
in flight.

The airplane factories want us.
They need workers, and they don't care
if we speak Spanish on the job. . . .

It's blasted over *la radio* every day, an invitation
to make more money than any cannery,
packing plant,
or farm
could ever offer,
by working like Rosie the Riveter
in that famous song, fusing metal to metal
with equipment that women never used
before this war
that has taken
all the men
far away.

Winged Dreams
Marisela

Is it TRUE,
that promise
on those
billboards?

Could my sister really BUILD
shiny, birdlike machines that will RISE up
toward the stars like magic,
WINNING
and
ENDING
this on-and-on series of battles?

While Lorena applies for a man's job,
I keep singing at union meetings,
but in between spells of real life,
I fly back toward daydreams
of dancing and LOVE.

When, *ay, cuándo*, will Manolito
return?

The Interview
Lorena

Men, women, a series of people
all asking such difficult questions.

Yes, I'm a citizen, hard worker, fluent reader.
I can follow directions in English, I do understand
that even tiny mistakes will cost lives
if airplanes
are made wrong,
so that they tumble down, down,
down from blue sky.

A beauty contest at the aircraft factory?
I say yes, yes, right in the middle of the most
confusing part of the interview, without
understanding that it's part of an official plan
for the city of Los Angeles to forget the riots.

If *mexicanas* are included in beauty, they explain,
then clearly everything is fair and equal,
even the past.

No School
Ray

Bored.
Battered with chores.
Nothing to do but work all day in the garden
for my grandma, who even makes me do laundry,
ironing, mending.
Girls' work.
Embarrassing.

Abuela tells me I should be ashamed,
avergonzado, for getting expelled
from *una escuela* that could have made **ME**
the first in our family to graduate
with the sort of education
old folks call
preparación.

Preparation—for what?
Does she really believe that I
could ever go to college
and get a good job?

Four-Four
Ray

After Abuela begs him, a shop teacher
talks the principal into bringing me back
to school
on the four-four plan, half a day
in classes, the other half
making bombs
for the war effort.

Industrial arts suddenly changes
from woodworking, welding, and auto repair
to mixing up chemicals, explosives,
DANGER.

But this four-four work-study program
seems like my ONLY chance to graduate
and make Papá *orgulloso*/proud
when he finishes
fighting.

My First Real Job
Ray

The four-four money comes in handy
for my family, but it means I have to spend
half of each day touching powders
designed
for death.

So I end up looking up at the SKY
after work, seeing—or IMAGINING—
the ghost
or angel
of José Díaz.

Sombra, fantasma, espíritu, espanto, muerto,
all the words I know for naming a dead guy
make me feel like I'm not quite completely
alive
yet.

Studying
Ray

It's not so bad.
Most of the words in my new English class
make sense.

Certain poems have a bold **RHYTHM**.
Others just quietly sing
and sway.

Math moves around in my mind too,
rows of numbers describing themselves
as one-at-a-time,
eventually mastered
tasks.

Solve this problem.
Carry the remainder.
Show every step.
Yes, it takes practice.
No, I don't have to make anything
look
easy.

GIRLS!
Ray

After school, after work,
girls ask me to dance in every contest,
even the **HUGE** competitions
in **ENORMOUS** sports stadiums.

Pachuco hop, that's what I dance best,
just casual and **COOL** while the girl glides
and spins all around me.

It's a style with its own NAME now, like breakaway
or swing out.

Pachuco hop—my privately, personally,
very-much-alive invented world.

I toss my partner up in the air, catch her,
and bring her back down from outer space
to Earth, so that together we almost always
WIN!

The Spirit of Ray
Ray

When peeled people
move into our own
swirls
and twirls
of meaning
we no longer
see ourselves
as ghostly.
I'm
ALIVE!
¡Viva la vida!

VICTORY
FAMILIA

November 1943

VICTORY

Sharing
Marisela

WHISPERING to other women
at work, I describe the fair treatment
we deserve—safe conditions,
reasonable hours, the same pay as men . . .
but at home, I'm not a union organizer,
just a helper for Abuela, kneading *masa*
to make tamales, so we can sell them
on Saturday mornings at church
to raise money for charities
that feed hungry refugees
overseas, in the horror
of Europe's
war zones.

When skinny children
from our own neighborhood
beg for scraps of broken tamales,
I hand them over, glad to be HELPING
in two places
at the same time!

Mariachi music.
I dance a polka, imagining Manolito

back in Cuba, all the letters I receive
filled with descriptions
of his own island's efforts
to keep Nazi submarines
from reaching
the U.S.

Portions of each sheet of paper
are blacked out by the pen
of a military censor.

He's joined Cuba's navy,
helping to escort American warships
across dangerous waters.

When I send careful answers
on perfumed paper, I have no way
of knowing whether the wild feelings
behind my cautious words
will be allowed
to travel.

El Día de los Muertos
Lorena

The Day of the Dead.
A reunion with family spirits right after—
but so different from—Halloween, a holiday of ghosts.

Marisela has union pamphlets at work
and Manolito's love letters at home,
but all I receive are these black-edged
death envelopes
that were handed out
at church.

Mami assigns me the task
of writing ancestral names—*los abuelos*
who lived long ago in México.

Ray tells me to add one more
black mourning note
for the spirit of José Díaz,
victim of murder.

So much time has passed
since I thought
about the violence at Sleepy Lagoon

that I feel like I'm dreaming
of a future, not the past.
Just one death?
What a relief that would be now,
while war news grows every day,
more and more gold stars
on our neighbors'
tragic windows.

With respect for my little brother's request,
I scribble the name of José, a stranger.

Fragrant incense at church,
mysterious Latin words
as the priest chants on and on,
until finally he places
the comfort
of a Communion wafer
on my peace-hungry tongue.
Then *pan del cielo*. Bread of heaven.
On *el Día de los Muertos*, I've always loved
swallowing tiny bites of mercy
for all the saints,

las ánimas, the spirits,
los angelitos,
little angels. . . .

Abuela says *los difuntos fieles*, the loyal dead,
will be grateful for all the toys, food, and flowers
that we carry to the cemetery for our picnic
with the ancestors,
but this year I'm not
doing it just for spirits,
it's also for the living,
Nicolás
and Papá. . . .

Relief
Abuela

Sometimes happiness is just
the momentary absence
of sadness.

No graves with the names of descendants,
just *los antepasados*
my ancestors.

Our celebration at the graveyard
is lively as we greet invisible
loved ones
from long ago,
sharing sugar skulls
and flowers of death,
the orange and yellow *flores*
called marigolds.

Do Memories Ever Leave Us Completely Alone?

Ray

Abuela tells me
that owls
and spirits
are invisible
in darkness,
mysterious
at dawn,
timid
in sunlight,
fearless
by twilight,
and happy at our picnic . . .
but she can't answer
any of my questions
about the future
of José Díaz
or the past
of my own
feelings.

A Free Country
Ray

As soon as our celebration with *los muertos*
is over, my thoughts turn from family spirits
to movement.

The Los Angeles City Council
might be able to forbid zoot suits,
but they can't outlaw **DANCING**,
can they?

After school, during work, while wondering
about questions no one can answer, I make up
my mind
to **LEAP**
as high as I can,
maybe even learn other steps someday—there's
a man named José Limón, who people say
makes modern dance look muscular and masculine
because he leaps so high that he seems to
FLY, ballet style, not zooter. . . .

Interviews
Marisela

Hat, suit, tie, notebook, pen,
camera . . .

At first glance, I assume
that the STRANGER at our door
is someone from work, a boss or checker
here to FIRE ME, but he turns out to be
a reporter, calling us *una familia*
de la victoria,
even though he can't
pronounce a single
Spanish syllable
correctly.

At least he's trying.
A VICTORY FAMILY, he explains,
describing his series of news articles
about people who contribute toward
the war effort
in so many quiet ways,
not just by fighting,
but by growing food in our garden,
donating blood to the Red Cross,

and working at jobs that support
the military.

It's confusing for me
to think of my cannery labor
as strategic, but it's true; the food
we send overseas is just as IMPORTANT
as Ray's
explosives.

What would this reporter say
if he knew that I'm secretly a union
organizer, determined to make LIFELONG
policies, not just temporary publicity
during these war years?

I imagine he wants only stories
about girls who OBEY
men's rules.

Beauty Contest
Lorena

I don't want to answer the reporter's
nosy questions about how it feels
to be a runner-up in the
Riveting Rosie Victory Competition.

I entered that tricky beauty pageant
because Mexican and Filipino girls
were encouraged to try, even though
our darker friends from Mississippi
and Alabama were falsely advised
that the competition
was already
full.

As it turns out, I'm just barely light enough
to be a Riveting Rosie princess, but never
the queen of an aircraft manufacturer's
shiny calendar.

By the time November
is pinned up on every wall
of the entire enormous factory,
my brown face has already

been spread all over Los Angeles
on billboards that announce
in many languages:
NOW HIRING!

Esta guerra es suya
Mami

This war is yours.
The nervous reporter
quotes a slick billboard.

No me importa.
I don't care.
No war is mine.
Women don't start wars.
All I want is my husband
and my son
home
alive.

¡Viva la victoria!
Long live victory!
Yes, he can photograph
my enthusiastic smile
when he repeats
his newspaper's
hopeful slogan.

Every Story Needs an Angle

Reporter #1

We're under orders
to make this city
seem unified.

Reporter #2

The riots made my reputation.
Now I owe it to this city to dig up
all these Spanish-talking war heroes
that the officials say we need
in order to keep
the peace
here at home.

Reporter #3

That older brother
is the real story.
MISSING IN ACTION!
The most powerful
headline
for my riveting new
Victory Family
AMALGAMATION
angle.

Amalgamation
Ray

The Victory *Familia* news story
comes out all mixed up
and full of nonsense
about how to fuse
different cultures
"without resorting
to intermarriage."

As soon as I have a chance,
I duck into the school library
to look up *amalgamation*
in a dictionary.

It means uniting one metal with another,
merging them into a single substance,
creating an alloy of poisonous mercury
with gold, silver, etc.

So what I want to know is, do newsmen
imagine that WE are the poison
or the gold?

Reality
Lorena

I keep certain aspects of my defense job
private.

That first day working inside the cockpit of a plane
I cried.

The noise of my rivet gun sounded
like danger.

Now I've gotten used to the size and noise
of the factory.

We're as big as a city,
one hundred thousand employees
rushing around
inside giant
windowless
buildings,
the whole thing
covered up
with camouflage nets
that are decorated
with fake canvas houses,

with brown-and-green wire trees
and painted streets to make it look—from above—
like a quiet neighborhood,
not a rooftop.

Illusions, just in case Los Angeles is seen
by enemy pilots who are trying
to bomb us.

Another illusion is the way we dress.
Women riveters wear men's pants
or overalls, our hair covered up
by kerchiefs, our feet protected
by rugged boots.

None of that beauty-contest fantasy
ever mattered—we come to work each day
looking
like our brothers.

Life Changes a Little Bit More
Every Day
Abuela

All the old ways are fading.
My own *abuelita* used herbs to cure fears,
brushing my skin with feathery branches
from a pirul pepper tree, then rubbing
my arms and legs with a cool
smooth
egg.

By the next day, any scary nightmare
from evil dreams would show up as a face
painted on the egg, hidden
under my bed,
where it couldn't harm me.

Now, when I listen to that "Rosie the Riveter" song
on *la radio*, I remember our old ways of dancing
that had nothing to do with girls acting tough,
unless we were singing *corridos*
about women who fought in the Mexican
Revolution—so I tell Lorenita, Don't worry,
it's fine to be strong, bold, brave!

La zooterina
Lorena

It's a decision I make all at once,
not slowly.

I don't even need to go to a clothing store,
because Ray still has a zoot suit he hardly ever
wears, now that he's so busy
studying,
studying,
studying.

This long, dark jacket is heavy,
the baggy black pants so floppy
that they might as well be a skirt.

Strutting into the factory
feels triumphant,
because I already know
that I'm a good worker,
well trained and efficient.

Even one tiny error could bring a plane
down, cause a crash, kill the pilot,
so my careful attention to detail
is essential.

Wearing a zoot suit on the job
shows what I think of the hypocritical
beauty contest.

My boss just glances at me
and shrugs.

I'm not the only *mexicana*
wearing drapes today.

We all agreed
that our brothers' clothes
deserve respect
and courage.

We're like the longtime *zooterinas*,
who adopted drapes years ago, just to show
that they're
rebellious.

Transformed

Ray

When I see one of my sisters
going to work in my **COOL** suit,
and the other making ¡*HUELGA*¡
STRIKE¡
signs
to march
in a picket line,
I start to feel like maybe
the girls I dance with
during school vacations
might also suddenly change
in **WEIRD** new ways,
but I don't really mind
because ¡*watcha*¡
I'm **CHANGING** too.

AMERICANOS ALL!

Epilogue

1948

Americanos All!

Nicolás

Segregated troops.
All the Mexicans were kept separate.
Yes, I resented it.
Then I was captured.
Prisoner of war.
Purple Heart.
Medal of Honor.

By the time I was found and freed,
Papá was already back here at home,
working as usual, all the rest of *la familia*
so proudly treating him
like an ordinary
everyday
hero
even though in Germany
he helped liberate starving people
from unbelievably cruel camps created
by unimaginably horrible levels
of arrogant racial
hatred.

Now the whole family sits here
by *la radio*, awaiting a verdict

for *Perez v. Sharp*, a California
Supreme Court test case
that will decide
whether a *mexicana* woman
can marry a black man.

It means everything to Marisela,
because if Pérez wins, then my lovestruck sister
will finally be able to marry the *cubano* musician
she met
during that wild
wartime
jazz craze.

He went away, but when he came back,
they started living together, and now . . .

I'm already far enough along
in my GI Bill–funded college classes
to be sure that the crazy old
anti-miscegenation law
is a clear violation
of the Fourteenth Amendment
to the United States Constitution,

which guarantees equal rights
for **ALL**, and that includes
intermarriage.

Man, it's hard to believe
that something so simple
wasn't already legal/*legal*—
one of those short, easy words
that looks exactly the same
in English and Spanish,
two languages that share
so many
Latin roots.

Pues, if I don't make it through law school,
maybe Lorena will, because when she lost
her fighter plane manufacturing job
at the end of the war, she went back
to school, and now we're both
on our way to changing
the way racially hateful people
are allowed to act, no matter
what they think.

Ray is still winning dance contests,
and Marisela says she's finally ready
to give up her job as a union organizer

and stay home with her baby
while Manolito plays his music
at the Palladium, the Million Dollar,
and other Hollywood
dance halls.

Sometimes when I look at the dry gray streets
of Los Angeles, I wonder what it would have been like
to twirl and leap
during the jazz craze,
when I was far away
and my hometown's
night sky
was a river
of music!

Author's Note

As a Cuban American child growing up in the Mexican American community of northeast Los Angeles during the 1950s, I was aware of a nearby armory where just a few years earlier, navy recruits had launched horrific attacks against Mexican American teenagers. Generally known as the Zoot Suit Riots, the violence could more accurately be referred to as the Sailor Riots.

Jazz Owls is a work of historical fiction, but the major events and situations were real, including the roles of police and journalists. All the characters in this story are entirely imaginary, with the exception of José Díaz, whose murder at Sleepy Lagoon led to an era so bizarre that while I was writing, I had to keep reminding myself that, yes, history really can be weird enough to make facts nearly impossible to believe.

In 1944 the Sleepy Lagoon convictions were overturned, and all the condemned young men were released. In 1948 the United States military was desegregated, and California's law against intermarriage was declared unconstitutional. During the 1960s, Mexican American leaders were at the forefront of California's nonviolent protests against the Vietnam War, as well as the movement that demanded fair treatment for agricultural workers. I think of those peaceful protesters as true heroes, whose profound courage was especially remarkable in the aftermath of such extremely violent racial oppression.

References

Escobedo, Elizabeth. *From Coveralls to Zoot Suits: The Lives of Mexican American Women on the World War II Home Front.* Chapel Hill: University of North Carolina Press, 2013.

Mazón, Mauricio. *The Zoot-Suit Riots.* Austin: University of Texas Press, 1984.

Pagán, Eduardo Obregón. *Murder at the Sleepy Lagoon: Zoot Suits, Race, and Riot in Wartime L.A.* Chapel Hill: University of North Carolina Press, 2003.

Pérez Firmat, Gustavo. *The Havana Habit.* New Haven, CT: Yale University Press, 2010.

Ponce, Mary Helen. *Hoyt Street.* Albuquerque: University of New Mexico Press, 2006.

Ruiz, Vicki L. *Cannery Women, Cannery Lives: Mexican Women, Unionization, and the California Food Processing Industry, 1930–1950.* Albuquerque: University of New Mexico Press, 1987.

Valdez, Luis. *Zoot Suit, and Other Plays.* Houston: Arte Público Press, 1992.

Acknowledgments

I thank God for nonviolent heroes.

Special thanks to Dr. Larissa Mercado-López, Justino Balderrama, Virginia Apodaca, Guadalupe García McCall, Sandra Garza, and David Bowles for proofreading, and to Rudy Gutiérrez for his magnificent illustrations.

I'm grateful to my wonderful agent, Michelle Humphrey, and my exquisite editor, Reka Simonsen, along with the whole incredibly supportive Atheneum/Simon & Schuster publishing team.

A Reading Group Guide to
Jazz Owls: A Novel of the Zoot Suit Riots
By Margarita Engle

Discussion Questions

1. How has the author organized this story and the information presented? What are the themes in the story? What are key features that help you understand the themes as well as the important ideas and details?

2. Throughout the book, the author chooses to use words in Spanish, words in different font sizes, words in bold and italics, and unconventional spacing. What is the purpose of formatting the text in this way? Does it help you in your understanding and reading of the book?

3. Describe the significance of music and dance to Mexican American youth during this time period. Where does the term Jazz Owls come from? Is this a good description?

4. What were the obstacles that Ray, Lorena, and Marisela had to face growing up in LA in wartime 1940s? Why

is this important to the story and these characters in particular? Consider time and place, setting, social pressures, and group dynamics.

5. Ray is a complex character who faces significant challenges over the course of the book. Name some of those challenges. How does Ray deal with them? What events and people cause him to change? What kind of information could you provide about Ray that would fill in the gaps that the author doesn't address?

6. Do you believe there is ever an appropriate time to use violence to resolve conflict? Has your reading of *Jazz Owls* influenced or changed your opinion?

7. How were the Zoot Suit Riots handled by the police? Do you agree or disagree with their actions? Do you think similar kinds of riots could happen today? What related desires, needs, and fears remain today?

8. Note the attitudes of the sailors and police along with their justifications of the riots and why they occurred. Why do you think these groups acted

in this way? What was your reaction to their justifications?

9. What role does the Sleepy Lagoon murder play in the Zoot Suit Riots? Do you think the riots would have occurred if the murder had not been committed?

10. In the United States, people are guaranteed a fair and equal trial, deemed innocent until proven guilty. What might have influenced the court and the sentencing of the 38th Street Gang in the Sleepy Lagoon murder?

11. Racial profiling existed in the 1940s. What are some current examples of racial profiling? Do you notice any differences between the racial profiling in *Jazz Owls* and the events of today's world? How do you think people can work to change stereotypes and unjust treatment?

12. Mexican American WWII veterans fought in the war to defend their country, the United States. After they returned home, they were discriminated against by the same people they fought alongside. How do you think these veterans

felt? How does the author give us insight into their feelings?

13. During the war, women started working in factories and occupying roles that men had traditionally filled. They were earning higher wages and taking on more responsibilities. How do you think women and girls felt at the end of the war as many of them returned to traditional homemaker roles after doing what was considered "men's work"? How does the author give us insight into their feelings?

Reading group guide written by Sharon Haupt, District Librarian, San Luis Coastal Unified School District.

This guide, written in alignment with the Common Core Standards (www.corestandards.org) has been provided by Simon & Schuster for classroom, library, and reading group use. It may be reproduced in its entirety or excerpted for these purposes.

Turn the page for a look
at Margarita Engle's next book:

ABANDONED

My first memory was one I could not understand
until years later: playing with towering animals
under a palm tree, all around me gentle eyes,
feathery green fronds,
and sticky tidbits of fruit
stuck to cow lips.

The cattle were smelly
and friendly,
just as hungry
for palm fruit
as I was
for milk.

Where did Mamá go?
I was too young for a sense of time,
but somehow I expected to be exiled forever
in that musical tangle of thumping hoofs
and clackety horns, my own wailing voice
adding a flute-like magic
to the noise.

LOST

When I remember abandonment,
all I feel is a sense of my smallness.

The roaming bulls ignored me.
I must have been too tiny
to seem
truly human.

Muddy legs, grubby face.
If I'd stayed in that cow world
long enough, I might have grown
hoofs, horns,
two more legs,
and a swishing tail.

WILD RHYMES

Jaguars, pumas, and other big cats,
poisonous snakes and vampire bats . . .

When Mamá abandoned me in a jungle,
did she think about all the fearful creatures
or was she merely offering me a green gift,
the sneaky hunt
for shy
sly
strangely
prowling
rhymes
to help me pass safely
through a dangerous
wilderness
called
time?

AM I AN ANIMAL YET?

With the rhythmic music of the herd
rattling through my busy mind,
I tried to moo like a cow,
coo like a dove,
then holler
and bellow,
just a lost and lonely little boy
whose human voice rose up
in an effort to transform
beastly
emotions.

No, I was not an animal,
but yes, I felt grateful
to four-legged creatures
for the lullabies they sang
to green trees
and blue sky.

Someday I will sing too,
instead of moaning.

FOUND

He was an angry farmer who spanked
my bottom.
Thwack!
Smack!
The crackling shuffle of rustling hoofs
sounded like a dance, as my cow-friends
saw their chance to escape, leaving me alone
with the shouting stranger
who tossed me across
a mule's broad back,
where I bumped and swayed
all the way
to a palm-thatched hut . . .

but Mamá was not there
in the little house.
She had gone
     away.

LIKE A BIRD

Black eyes.
Slender hands.
Dark hair.
Waterfall laughter.

Trying to picture
my lost mother
has become a race
of entrancing words
that gallop
faster
and faster.

Did Mamá fly into the sky
like a winged being,
or is she alive
and hiding?

BIG MOUTH

A bearded man on a spirited horse
rescued me from the gloomy farmer.

We thundered far across the green hills
of Honduras, hoof beats making me feel
like a centaur, as we galloped over the border
to Nicaragua—my homeland—but not
to the small room in the back of a store
in the little town of Metapa
where I was born.

Instead, we ended up in a rambling old
horseshoe-shaped house in the city of León,
where I was finally told that Mamá wanted me
to live HERE
with strangers.

I soon learned that the bearded rescuer
was my great-uncle, called El Bocón
by all who knew him.

Big Mouth, such a suitable nickname
for a man who tells tall tales
in a booming, larger-than-life
story voice.

He speaks of steep mountains with icy peaks,
and of gallant knights who battle ogres and dragons,
and of smoothly rolling hills in distant lands,
countries so remote
and amazing
that I can hardly absorb
the fascinating range
of exotic names.

Has he really traveled so much?
France? California?

Soon, when I grow up,
I plan to roam the earth
and be a Big Mouth too,
speaking truthfully
whenever I choose,
never caring
if anyone
is offended.

Any harsh fact is so much better
than telling lies like a tricky mother
who pretends
she'll just be gone
for a little while.

ADOPTED

El Bocón and his wife,
my great-aunt Bernarda,
decide to make me their son.

He's huge and loud, she's small and flowery,
with curly hair, a delicate voice,
and an eager way of making children
join all her songs, parties,
and prayers.

Living in their vast, echoing home,
I soon learn the essential skill of storytelling
along with horsemanship, hunting, fishing,
and wild fruit harvesting.

The only art I never master
is convincing others that I don't really care
how
and why
Mamá vanished.

SO MANY STORYTELLERS

The city is musical
with church bells
and chirping birds,
heels tapping
on cobblestones,
and lush green gardens
that grow so fast that every morning
brings new blossoms, each with its own
enchanted fragrance.

El Bocón is not the only one who fills
the humid air
with ribbons of words
that seem to draw pictures. . . .

Serapia is the cook who tells tales she learned
from her africano ancestors, and Goyo the gardener
speaks of our shared native heritage,
my brown skin and black hair
just as indio as his.

Was Mamá a mestiza of half-Matagalpan descent,
or did she belong to the Pipil Nahua,
Maya, Chontal, Niquirano, Chorotega,
Miskito, or some other proud forest nation?

When I sit in church, the stories I hear

are even more improbable than El Bocón's
fanciful tales of foreign lands.

The priest speaks of a man
swallowed by a fish,
a boy with a slingshot
who battles a giant,
burning bushes,
and a talking donkey—but no one
ever mentions children left behind
in cow pastures, so maybe reality
is the strangest,
most mystery-filled
terrible
true story
of all.

WINNER OF THE 2015 PURA BELPRÉ AWARD ANI 2016 WALTER DEAN MYERS HONOR AWARD

FOR OUTSTANDING CHILDREN'S LITERATURE

*Each time we fly back to our everyday
lives, one of my two selves
is left behind. . . .*

IN THIS HAUNTINGLY BEAUTIFUL MEMOIR, Newbery Honor–winner Margarita Engle tells of growing up with two cultures during a time of cold hostility between the United States and Cuba, and of the childhood that shaped this sensitive young girl into an award-winning poet.

"This is a book to return to, page after page, line after line. Exquisite."

—Kathi Appelt, author of Newbery Honor and National Book Award finalist *The Underneath*

✷ "Beautifully told."

—*Kirkus Reviews,* starred review

✷ "[A] worthy addition to any collection."

—*Booklist*, starred review

atheneum